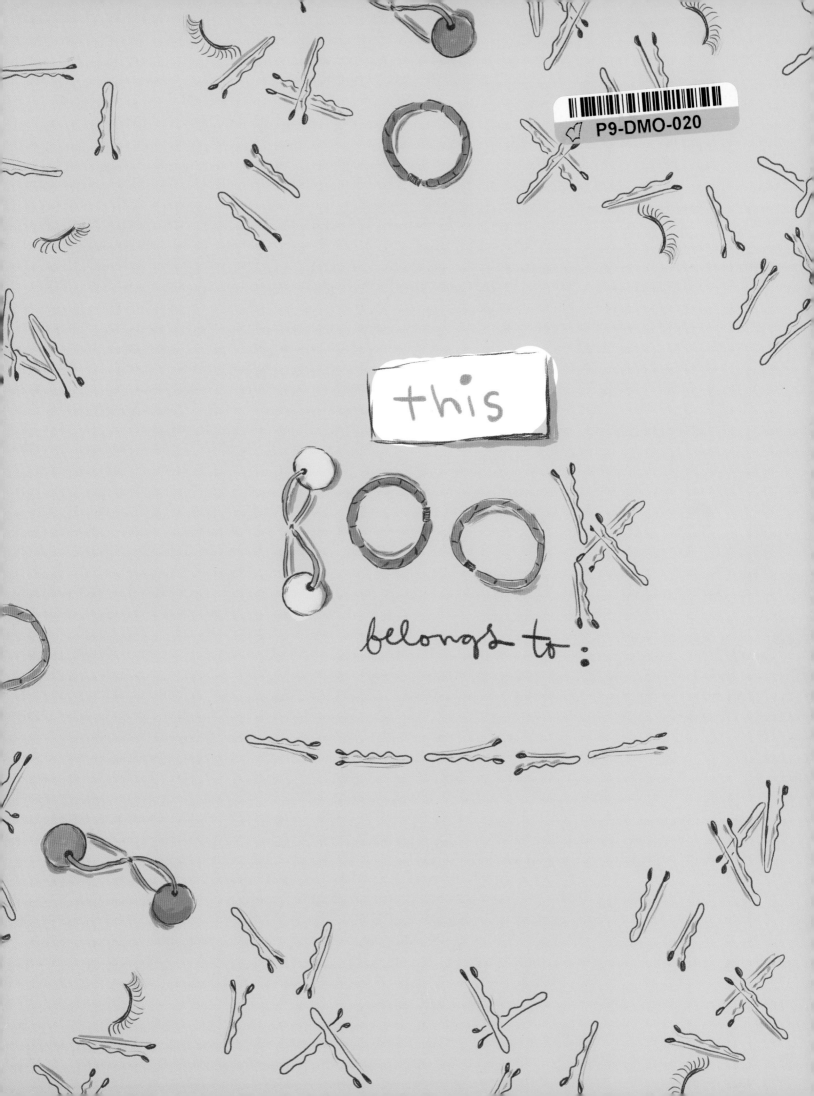

this

book

belongs to:

_____

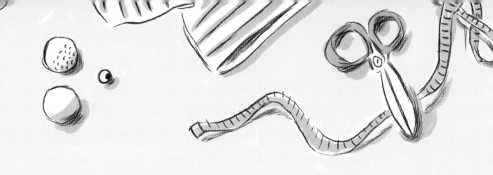

For my sisters—
Michelle, Deanna, Jennell, Kelly, and Kelly
—K. D.

For Beatrix
—H. R.

ATHENEUM BOOKS FOR YOUNG READERS
An imprint of Simon & Schuster Children's Publishing Division
1230 Avenue of the Americas, New York, New York 10020
Text copyright © 2013 by Kelly DiPucchio
Illustrations copyright © 2013 by Heather Ross
All rights reserved, including the right of reproduction in whole or in part in any form.
ATHENEUM BOOKS FOR YOUNG READERS is a registered trademark of Simon & Schuster, Inc.
Atheneum logo is a trademark of Simon & Schuster, Inc.
For information about special discounts for bulk purchases, please contact Simon &
Schuster Special Sales at 1-866-506-1949 or business@simonandschuster.com.
The Simon & Schuster Speakers Bureau can bring authors to your live event. For more
information or to book an event, contact the Simon & Schuster Speakers Bureau at
1-866-248-3049 or visit our website at www.simonspeakers.com.
Book design by Lauren Rille
The text for this book is set in Skizzors.
The illustrations for this book are rendered in pencil, then colored digitally.
Manufactured in China
0513 SCP
First Edition
2 4 6 8 10 9 7 5 3 1
Library of Congress Cataloging-in-Publication Data
DiPucchio, Kelly S.
Dress-up mess-up / by Kelly DiPucchio ; illustrations by Heather Ross. — 1st ed.
p. cm. — (Crafty Chloe)
Summary: After telling each of her best friends that her costume
for the Parade of Books will match theirs, Chloe must come up with a crafty way
of making Leo, Emma, and herself happy.
ISBN 978-1-4424-2124-0
ISBN 978-1-4424-4391-4 (eBook)
[1. Costume—Fiction. 2. Handicraft—Fiction. 3. Best friends—Fiction. 4. Friendship—Fiction.
5. Parades—Fiction.] I. Ross, Heather, ill. II. Title.
PZ7.D6219Dre 2013
[E]—dc23   2011042345

Crafty CHLOE

DRESS-UP MESS-UP

by
KELLY DiPUCCHIO

illustrations by
HEATHER ROSS

ATHENEUM BOOKS FOR YOUNG READERS
New York London Toronto Sydney New Delhi

Chloe closed her book. "Awesome!" she shouted.

"I knew it!" cried Leo. "I knew the treasure was hidden in the haunted cave!"

Chloe loved the Monster Mystery books. Her friend Leo did too. The Parade of Books was next week at school, and they had been planning their costumes for weeks.

Chloe was going to be Frankenstein.

Leo was going to be Dracula.

And Chloe's baby brother,
pictured here . . .

and here . . .

and here . . .

was going to be in VERY BIG trouble if he didn't stay out of Chloe's stuff!

Chloe groaned. "*This* little monster is not invited to our next book club meeting," she told Leo.

The following day Chloe went to Emma's house for their weekly spa day. Emma painted her toenails.

Chloe painted posters for the parade.

The Parade of Books
A MOST Favorite DAY

"We should be Fairy Club fairies!"

Emma squealed, looking at the poster. "I'll be Twinkle and you can be Shimmer!"

The Parade of Books
A MOST Favorite
DAY

Emma's eyes were shiny and happy, like two round sequins. Chloe bit down on the end of her paintbrush, not sure what to say.

"What's wrong?" Emma asked.
"I thought you liked Shimmer."

"I do. But . . ."

"But what?"

"Well, I was thinking . . ."
Chloe paused and then dabbed
a blob of green paint on her nose.
"I was thinking it might be fun to be *Frankenstein* this year!"

"You're going to be a MONSTER?!"

Emma's oatmeal mask cracked.

Chloe's cheeks turned the color of Emma's nail polish. "I'm sorry. That was rude," Emma said softly. "You can be whoever you want to be."

Now Emma's eyes were shiny and sad, like two brown buttons. Chloe sighed. "But Shimmer might be kind of fun too."

"Thank goodness!" Emma said cheerfully, placing a crown of flowers on Chloe's head. "You had me worried! The Fairy Club books are the best! This is going to be *so* perfect!"

Chloe forced a smile.
"Yep," she said with a nod. "Perfect."

That afternoon Chloe admired her Frankenstein jacket.
It had taken her weeks to sew the patches on.
Why didn't she just tell Emma the truth?

Chloe spent the next two
hours making fairy wings.

The first pair was too FLOPPY.

The second, too FLUFFY!

But the third pair was JUST RIGHT.

In fact, they were the most magical fairy wings Chloe had ever made in her whole entire life! Maybe this would be fun after all.

Bert barked.

LEO!

Chloe had forgotten all about Leo!
What would she tell him?

Hmm . . . maybe she could convince
Leo to be the fairy king?
Bert made a face.

"You're right," Chloe agreed.
"That will never happen."

Chloe tried to picture
Emma dressed as a monster.

"Never in a million years,"
she whispered sadly.

The next morning Chloe sprang out of bed.
"Problem solved!" she announced to Sock Monkey.
"I'm not going to be a monster or a fairy!"

Sock Monkey listened closely to this breaking news.

"I'm going to be a completely different character," Chloe explained. "That way I won't have to choose between Leo and Emma!"

Chloe went through her craft supplies and books.

A cowgirl? Maybe.

A pirate? Possibly.

A porcupine ninja? Maybe not.

"Problem *not* solved," she complained. "How am I supposed to pick ONE favorite book? That's like picking ONE favorite crayon out of a box of one hundred and twenty. It's too much to ask!"

Later that day Chloe went to the park with her family.

"Chloe, why are you wearing your winter coat and hat?" her father asked.

Chloe looked up at the sky. "Because I'm pretty sure we're going to have a snow day at school tomorrow."

Chloe's father choked on his coffee.

Chloe's mother lifted up her sunglasses to look at the blue sky.

Chloe's baby brother put a bucket on his head.

And Bert, pictured here . . .

and here . . .

and here . . .

was busy trying to get the
ice-cream man's attention.

"Chloe, it's seventy-five degrees outside," her father pointed out.

"Well, I, for one, hope school isn't canceled," her mother announced. "The Parade of Books is tomorrow. Isn't that one of your most favorite days, Chloe?"

Chloe shrugged. "I like snow days better."

"Grandma would be disappointed," Chloe's mother said. "She looks forward to going to the parade and seeing your costume every year."

Chloe began to sweat.

There was no snow and no costume, but there was no way she was going to disappoint Grandma, too. Chloe unzipped her coat and sat down to think.

When Chloe got home
she went straight to work.

Fussing

and fixing.

Measuring

and mixing.

That night Chloe was so excited, she could hardly sleep. She thought her costume was the best new creation since scented Magic Markers! But what would Leo and Emma think?

On Monday morning the Parade of Books began after the first bell. The halls were packed with pirates and princesses, wizards and witches.

Leo looked frightfully scary.

Emma looked delightfully airy.

And Chloe?

Chloe looked happy to have two best friends who
thought she was the best airy,
scary, one-of-a-kind . . .

FRANKENFAIRY!

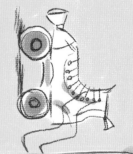

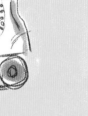

Do you like to make things too?
Visit me at
craftychloe.com

to learn how to make the
cool crafts featured
in this book.
See you there!